Bootsie BARKER BITES

BARBARA BOTTNER

ILLUSTRATED BY
PEGGY RATHMANN

A TRUMPET CLUB SPECIAL EDITION

ISBN 0-590-12923-6

Text copyright © 1992 by Barbara Bottner.
Illustrations copyright © 1992 by Peggy Rathmann.
All rights reserved. Published by Scholastic Inc., 555 Broadway, New York, NY 10012, by arrangement with G. P. Putnam's Sons, a division of The Putnam & Grosset Group.

TRUMPET and associated logos are trademarks and/or registered trademarks of Scholastic Inc.

12 11 10 9 8 7 6 5   1 2/0

Printed in the U.S.A.   **14**

Book design by Nanette Stevenson.
Lettering by David Gatti.
The text is set in Garamond Antiqua.

To Gerald, and Carole Horowitz, of course
—BB

To Barney Saltzberg, for whom even shy children sing
—PR

My mother and Bootsie Barker's mother are best friends.

When Mrs. Barker comes to visit, she always brings chocolate donuts, fresh strawberries, and Bootsie.

First, we have a tea party.
Then, my mother tells Bootsie and me
to play in my room.

I try to get Bootsie interested in my book about
turtles, but Bootsie hates turtles.

"*You're* a turtle!" howls Bootsie. "And *I'm* a
TURTLE-EATING DINOSAUR!"

My mother calls, "Play nicely, girls!"
Bootsie yells, "We are!"
I can't yell anything.

It's time for the Barkers to go home.

"We'll be back tomorrow!" says Mrs. Barker cheerfully.

I tell my mother I don't like playing with Bootsie Barker.

My mother tells me I have to learn to get along with all kinds of people.

I go to bed and dream that Mrs. Barker moves far
away and takes Bootsie with her.

But, Mrs. Barker and Bootsie never go anywhere
except the park, the grocery store,

and our house.
   "It's so nice you girls
can be friends," says Mrs.
Barker, as Bootsie leads
me to my room.

I let Bootsie look at my pet salamander,
Charlene.

But Bootsie hates salamanders.
"*You're* a salamander," screams Bootsie,
"and *I'm* a SALAMANDER-EATING
DINOSAUR!"

Mrs. Barker knocks on the bedroom door. It's time
for Bootsie to go home.

"Tomorrow," says Bootsie, "you get to be a worm."

That night, I dream that Bootsie accidentally falls
off the edge of the world.
 I try to save her, but it's too late.

In the morning, my mother says she has a wonderful surprise! Bootsie will be staying overnight at our house while her parents are in Chicago.

I picture Charlene and me being rushed to the
hospital with dinosaur bites.

When my mother asks me what Bootsie and I would like for snacks, I can't stand it anymore.

"Bootsie Barker is a DINOSAUR!" I shout, "and she's PLANNING TO EAT ME ALIVE!"

My mother looks surprised.

"Sweetheart," she says, "tell Bootsie you don't want to play that game."

I go to my room to think it over.

Charlene and I spend the morning inventing a
new game.

The doorbell rings. It's the Barkers dropping off
Bootsie-the-dinosaur.

"Hello, little worm!" says Bootsie.

I stand up and look Bootsie in the eye.
"Pardon me, Bootsie!
I am not a worm.
I am a PALEONTOLOGIST!
Do you know what *they* do?
They hunt for DINOSAUR bones.
Would *you* like to play?"

Bootsie runs out the front door.

She wants to go with her parents.

Mrs. Barker says Bootsie will have more fun if she stays at our house. Bootsie throws a tantrum on the sidewalk.

So Bootsie's parents take Bootsie to Chicago.

Which means I don't have to wish Bootsie takes a rocket to outer space.

Although if she does, it's fine with me.